Series 401

A Ladybird Book

This delightfully illustrated story, told in verse, describes the mischievous pranks of two lively kittens, SMOKE and FLUFF, and how their naughtiness was forgiven, in the end, by their understanding mother.

This book, and the companion titles listed on the back cover, will make an instant appeal to all young children.

SMOKE and FLUFF

Story and illustrations by A. J. MACGREGOR
Revised verses by W. PERRING

Ladybird Books Loughborough

Mrs. Cat was busy knitting,

Didn't notice soon enough

Kittens underneath the table,

Saucy Smoke and frisky Fluff.

Didn't see their little antics

    With the wool, as more and more—

Yards and yards of it were twisted

    Round the table, on the floor.

But at last it stopped her knitting!

Then she rose and gave a pull;

Said, " Oh dear ! What *can* have happened ?

Where's my ball of knitting wool ? "

Smoke and Fluff had softly vanished!

Mummy tugged again and frowned.

Tug! And over went the table,

With the tea-things to the ground.

What a sight upon the carpet!

Broken china, milk and tea!

Off upstairs the kittens scampered,

Did not dare to stay and see!

Here they spied a handy cupboard:

    Smoke said, " Quick, Fluff! In you go! "

Quick as lightning, in they darted,

    Fluff above and Smoke below!

Then they heard, with hearts abeating,

Mummy's footsteps drawing near!

Listened, breathless, as she ... passed them!

Peeped to see if all was clear.

Mummy vanished round the corner:

Out the naughty kittens came,

Not at all ashamed or sorry,

Ready for another game.

Down the stairs, the creeping couple

Through the open kitchen door

Saw the tarts upon the table,

Just what they were looking for !

In the kitchen, Cook was busy
    At the oven with her pie,
Didn't notice Smoke was peeping,
    With a gleaming, hungry eye.

Soft they stole across the kitchen :

　　Smoke was soon upon the bag,

Passed the tarts to Fluff, a-tiptoe !

　　But the sack began to sag !

Then there came the great disaster!

Down went sack and kittens all!

Burst the sack and clouds of flour

Scattered round them in their fall!

Startled at the sudden noises,

Cook could only stand and stare

At the fleeing kits, but did not

Recognise the guilty pair!

When she found the tarts had vanished,

    Cook was very, very cross,

Calling in alarm and anger,

    Thinking thieves had caused the loss.

Meanwhile, Smoke and Fluff were troubled;

Jane was kneeling at the door!

Upstairs, Mother, busy searching;

Cook behind and Jane before!

Then the kittens acted boldly,

Made a sudden flying leap

Over Jane and over bucket!

Tasty tarts they meant to keep!

As the couple scampered past her,

    Jane was startled, jumped in fright,

Knocked her water bucket over!

    Smoke and Fluff shot out of sight.

Cook and Jane were in a temper,

    Searched the garden high and low,

Muttered threats and asked each other,

    '' Where did those two rascals go ? ''

When at last they neared the tool shed,

    As they hunted through the grounds,

" Listen, Cook ! " said Jane, excited,

    " Do you hear some funny sounds ? "

There, within, they saw the kittens

    Munching tarts without a care !

Winking, Cook exclaimed quite loudly,

    " Now we've caught the naughty pair ! "

Smoke and Fluff at last were frightened :

Dropped the tarts and leapt again,

This time making for the window,

Once more to escape ! . . . In vain !

Smoke was half way through the window,

Little dreaming who was there,

Till he saw that Cook was waiting,

In her eye a steely glare!

Caught at last, the little rascals

    Filled the air with sorry cries.

"*We're* not burglars!" wailed the kittens,

    As they sadly rubbed their eyes.

Safe at home, when Jane had scrubbed them,
  —And she scrubbed them hard enough,
For they had been very naughty—
  Shamed at last were Smoke and Fluff.

But their Mother soon forgave them,
  Understood their point of view;
For, like other people's children,
  Kittens will be kittens, too!